Dear Parents and Educators,

Welcome to Penguin Young Readers! As parents and educators, you know that each child develops at his or her own pace—in terms of speech, critical thinking, and, of course, reading. Penguin Young Readers recognizes this fact. As a result, each Penguin Young Readers book is assigned a traditional easy-to-read level (1–4) as well as a Guided Reading Level (A–P). Both of these systems will help you choose the right book for your child. Please refer to the back of each book for specific leveling information. Penguin Young Readers features esteemed authors and illustrators, stories about favorite characters, fascinating nonfiction, and more!

A Pig, a Fox, and Stinky Socks

LEVEL 2

GUIDED READING LEVEL **I**

This book is perfect for a **Progressing Reader** who:
- can figure out unknown words by using picture and context clues;
- can recognize beginning, middle, and ending sounds;
- can make and confirm predictions about what will happen in the text; and
- can distinguish between fiction and nonfiction.

Here are some **activities** you can do during and after reading this book:
- Rhyming Words: On a separate piece of paper, make a list of all the rhyming words in this story. For example, *pail* rhymes with *mail*, so write those two words next to each other.
- Compare/Contrast: In this book, we find out that Fox is little and Pig is big. In what other ways are they different? What do they have in common?

Remember, sharing the love of reading with a child is the best gift you can give!

—Sarah Fabiny, Editorial Director
Penguin Young Readers program

*Penguin Young Readers are leveled by independent reviewers applying the standards developed by Irene Fountas and Gay Su Pinnell in *Matching Books to Readers: Using Leveled Books in Guided Reading*, Heinemann, 1999.

For Mima, Papa, Grandma, and Grandpa—JF

PENGUIN YOUNG READERS
An Imprint of Penguin Random House LLC

Penguin supports copyright. Copyright fuels creativity, encourages diverse voices,
promotes free speech, and creates a vibrant culture. Thank you for buying an authorized edition
of this book and for complying with copyright laws by not reproducing, scanning, or distributing any
part of it in any form without permission. You are supporting writers and allowing Penguin to
continue to publish books for every reader.

Copyright © 2017 by Jonathan Fenske. All rights reserved. Published by Penguin Young Readers,
an imprint of Penguin Random House LLC, 345 Hudson Street, New York, New York 10014.
Manufactured in China.

Library of Congress Cataloging-in-Publication Data is available.

ISBN 9780515157802 (pbk)   10 9 8 7 6 5 4 3 2 1
ISBN 9780515157819 (hc)   10 9 8 7 6 5 4 3 2 1

A PIG, A FOX, AND STINKY SOCKS

by Jonathan Fenske

Penguin Young Readers
An Imprint of Penguin Random House

PART ONE

This pair of socks
was on my feet.

This pair of socks does
NOT smell sweet.

And hide inside
this handy pail.

To watch Pig find
his stinky mail.

These socks do not go in my MAIL.

They go inside my LAUNDRY PAIL.

LAUNDRY

12

13

PART TWO

18

Another pair of socks that stink.
Another funny trick I think.

19

21

Here comes Pig!
I must be quick!

This empty can
should do the
trick.

GARBAGE

22

I would not EVER want to eat the socks from Fox's stinky feet!

Uh-oh.

GARBAGE

26

27

And so does Fox.

28

PART THREE